Dedication

I want to dedicate this book to Greg Delaney, Bruce Lee, and Robert Davis who pushed me to make my poetry public, to read my poetry at open mic nights, and further more to push me to write this book. I never considered myself a poet before I was just a girl who wrote poetry. You all saw some of my work and pushed me to make it what I didn't even foresee it could ever be. I appreciate you in believing in me and pushing me to have my poetry not just heard but to give it the voice it has always given to me.

Thank You

~~~~Be my friend before you are my lover.
Get my heart before you get in my bed.
And I promise I'll be the best you've ever had.

Yours Truly,
April Stone

~~~I am not a "Bad Bitch". I am a beautiful Phenomenal
Woman.

Yours Truly,
April Stone

PART ONE

The Inner Thoughts of Life

Adam's Rib

A woman was made from the side of her man.
To not walk in front or behind him, but to walk beside him.
Go to war for him and with him in the battlefield, coming out strong every time.
You were made from his body so when you come together you form a union as one.
When you lay on his chest your heart beats are the same.
It's his warmth, his power, his love running through your veins.
Together you ignite a level of passion that you can't have with any other.
You were made from his side, your ribs are his ribs, and your bones are his bones.
Every part of you was made from him.
Without him you couldn't even exist.
Sorry sweetie from the day you were born you were never independent.
So many people go through countless relationships because they can't find "that one".
When you find that one, you always wonder how the feelings came so fast, so strong.
It's because he completes you, you complete him.
You were made from him, for him, from the side of your man.

Goodnight Kiss

Somewhere in a different lifetime you are my husband, I am your wife.
You are my king, I am your queen.
We are Adam and Eve.
We have a family and you are sitting on the couch watching football while I'm cooking you and the kids' dinner.
Then we end our night in our huge elegant bed, making love to each other until we fall asleep.
Looking in each other's eyes.
The last thing we say is I love you; you give me a kiss on my forehead, and say good night.

Love

Love is red, it's vibrant and amazing.
It sounds like a police car, sirens blasting while speeding down the street.
It smells like a fresh bouquet of fresh flowers.
It tastes like a cold glass of your favorite drink full of ice on a hot summer day.

Unconditional Love

To love someone unconditionally is the greatest love you can ever find.
It's amazing, satisfying, the most joyful feeling you can ever have.
But then again the pain from loving unconditionally is the saddest, most hurtful pain your heart can have.
The overwhelming feeling from the good times will make you cry.
The laughter, smiles, goofiness, bad jokes, those intimate times are the best moments in your life.
To take your hand as you take mine.
Loving each other through all our faults, past our pain.
I am yours and you are mine through eternity.
Unconditional love through the test of time.

Definition of Sexy

You're the sexiest man I've ever known.
Beautiful eyes, sexiest voice in the world.
The most beautiful skin tone.
You're more than just sexy and fine, you are a beautiful man, the best eye candy to any woman's eyes.
You walk into a room and all eyes are on you, you're so humble about it that makes it that much more of an attractiveness about you.
Your hair is fine, trimmed straight, line cut up every time.
When you speak, your deep base in your voice fills the presence in any room.
When you sing the sounds flow out of your mouth, so soft, tender, sexy, the best voice in the world, a voice from heaven indeed.
I sit back and watch and see how all the girls want you, I can't blame them I want you too.
You're tall and strong as ever.
Big arms, big shoulders, a sexy body, a body of a real man.
When you hold a woman, she just melts in your arms.
You're the sexiest man I've ever known.
From your sexy hair, to your nicely trimmed beard line.
Your beautiful face, those amazing eyes.
From your strong neck, where your shoulders are so big and strong.
Your back, a back like a real man, a back that can hold its own.
Your arms long and big that connect to those hands that are so strong.
The love you make is better than any man I've ever known.
Your cradle me with all your protection, my protector; it's the sexiest thing I know.
Emotionally, physically, sexually, you're the definition of sexy.
You are the sexiest man I've ever known.

Black Treasure

Before you knew it, I knew it for you.
You are a beautiful black man, every woman's treasure.
Strong hard working, fine as ever.
The qualities in a man every woman prays to God for.
I saw you when the other had you, the things I know about you, you didn't have to tell me.
I saw what you still don't know, and what they could never see.
Your big strong hands wrapping your arms around me.
Just the feeling in your arms, a feeling that only a real man can give me.
See any man can hold you, but not any man can wrap his arms around you, and with that his attentiveness, his protectiveness flows from his heart down through is his arms, from his arms to his fingertips, the fingertips that touch my skin that wraps my body tight.
That's a black treasure.
They couldn't see all that, and you didn't know it ether.
Not every woman can see that when a man works hard, that doesn't just show a good quality. It shows he's not just working hard for him; he's working hard for his family.
Even if he doesn't have on yet, he knows he will one day, so he knows to be good for them he has to provide, he has to be good for himself first. That is why a good man works so hard.
That's a quality of a black treasure.
See I saw you long before you knew it. I recognized the black treasure in you; you didn't have to wine and dine me to win me over. I knew having you would mean I was striking gold, I knew I had a black treasure and I had to get him.
Each kiss, each hug, each look from your eyes, and when you hit the bedroom it's like heaven every time.
See like any gem, ruby, or diamond you are precious too.
You need to be appreciated, treated like gold, and most of all treated like a king.
I hope one day I'm able to show you what a great black man you are. How a good man needs to be treated. Every woman prays to God to send them a man, a man that is exactly you.

You are right in front of my face and you don't even know it.
One day hopefully I can show you.
Hopefully, you will be my black treasure.

Our Babies

Bruised, battered, beaten, hungry, and unloved.
My heart cries out for you.
The mother in me just wants to pick you up and hold you.
Rescue you with food, shelter, and love.
Now I know why the sky cries.
Why earth is round and nature is a mother, why it rains so hard when God cries.
The earth wraps its body around you.
Mother Nature tries to protect you.
My heart is full of nothing but sadness; my eyes can't stop crying when I think of you.
I pray for you every night.
God please let them not go hungry, not be cold, abused, let them have somewhere safe to lay there head tonight.
Please let them feel unconditional love that our children do.
I wish I had the means to take care of each and every one of you.
Bruised, beaten, hungry, and unloved.
Children of this world, as a mother I cry for you.

So Gone

You had your chance and you didn't want it.
I gave you all of me and you still said no.
Why is it so hard for me to let you go?
You have moved on and done your thing.
Still come back to me from time to time when you want me.
To you I still run.
I still sit here waiting.
Still trying to hold on to what could be.
Still trying to prove to you I'm the one that can make you happy.
I'm smarter than this I know it won't happen, it will never be.
I was right in front of your face but still you were looking for love with someone other than me.
You didn't want me then or now, but still I can't leave.
When I get the courage up I feel sorry for you because then I'll be so gone, and then I'll be able to leave.
While you're still searching for love, I'll have a true love, an unconditional love that has just been waiting for me to stop loving you, so he could love me.

Truth Is Out

I fell in love with you, I did there's no denying that.
I can't take it back now and I can't help it.
Don't hold me in your arms at night.
Done whisper in my ear, don't hold me tight.
Stop telling me you love me, stop the lies.
Hush your mouth; don't let the words of unspoken truth
come out.
I found out your lie, you don't really love me.
That's your truth...it's out.

Unbreakable

No matter how much you try you can't break me.
You might come close, but you still won't.
I am as strong as I am beautiful.
I am not easily broken.

Words Are Golden

Fought for it, begged and pleaded.
So I gave it to you, gave you me heart wide open.
I had nothing but your word you would protect it.
Your word.
You took my hand and held me close, you made sure I
didn't let go.
You took my face, held it in your hands.
Looked me dead in my eye and told me you loved me, and told me
you cared.
You had me, my heart wide open.
I had nothing but your word you would protect it.
Your word.
They say sticks and stones will break your bones but words
will never hurt me.
When your words turned into lies.
Your words cut deep, crushed my heart with so much pain.
Your eyes looking me in mine while you pierced me like a
knife.
I had nothing but your word you would protect it.
Now I look you dead in your eye and please hear the words
I say to you.
I wish I never met you, let you have the pieces of me I gave
to you.
Pieces I held dear that were precious, pieces you were
supposed to protect.
Listen to my words, your word isn't shit, and I'm done
listening.

For Our Grandfather

They say gone but never forgotten.
Still in our presence.
Still in our hearts.
To them you may be physically gone, but to us you are still here.
You bring meaning to the phrase; you are never as old as your age, you are as young as you act and feel.
I was never blessed to have a grandfather of my own until you came into my life.
Me and WyDale could have never asked for a better grandfather for our children.
You have touched so many; my words could never say your entire worth.
In your lifetime to many you were and will always be:
a man sent from heaven, a friend, a father, a husband, provider, protector, teacher, a true man of honor, our grandfather.
To me, WyDale, Mylon, Tre', and Mya you are the greatest man we know.
You are our grandfather; the word itself is as strong as its meaning
A relationship that is so special only you and your grandchildren will ever know.
G-the godliness that lives in you.
R-the repeated love you continue to show.
A-always there no matter what.
N-never let go.
D-doer, you do whatever it takes to make sure your family is together and strong.
F-the great father that you are.
A-awesome is what your grand kids call you.
T-a teacher with wisdom and knowledge that you graciously show.
H-holy is what you are.
E-everlasting is what your love will always be.
R-you are the reflection of what God made a man to be.
GRANDFATHER
Each of us will take with us something special from you.
Something you've either done or said something precious we only share with you.

I will never forget what you told me.
Every time I think of you it comes to my head.
It was and still is the greatest compliment I could ever get.
You said you wished you could have met a woman like me when you were younger, you would have married me in a second.
Thank you grandpa.
I will still watch our football game with you Oklahoma vs. KState.
Maybe one day you'll beat KSU.
Our plans we always sat and talked about.
You and WyDale going on your fishing trip, you and the kids going on a road trip in the RV, on my wedding day, you dancing with me.
I need you, WyDale, and our babies to know our plans are not cancelled they are just a little postponed.
WyDale and the kids will still get there trips with you, and I will still dance with you on my wedding day.
Our plans now will just be at a different time, they will be in a much more beautiful place.
We will forever take with us your smile, your teachings, your laughter, your talks, your kindness, and most of all, your love.
Still in our hearts.
Still in our presence.
To them you may be physically gone, but to us you are still here.
To them you may be friend, father, and brother in Christ.
To us we get to be selfish and have the privilege to call you grandfather.
A relationship that we get to hold special, we get to hold dear.
Our grandfather to have and to hold. Sacred, for the rest of our lives.

The One

Be the one to wipe away my tears.
Stop me before I cry.
Hold me until that last tear drops from my eye.
Be the one to never leave.
Hold me strong, hold me tight.
Protect my heart, never hurt me, never be the one to make me cry.
Be the one to take away the dark lonely nights.

Wife Me

I want to be your wife.
To have and to hold, sickness and health.
Never divorce, only death could break us apart.
A love made from heaven, you were made just for me.
You my Adam me your Eve
My protector and provider, best friend until the end.
The one I run to, the one who gives me joy.
There is no other that could ever compare to the feeling
you give.
A love like yours people never find, it just doesn't happen.
Hold me in your in your arms, keep me safe, protect me
and never let me go.
To bare your children, have your last name is such an
honor.
Take my hand put it in yours; lead me as my man into a
love for eternity, a love for all time.
To conquer the world as you my husband, me your wife.

Thoughts of You Sleeping

Since the day I saw you, I knew I wanted you.
Your swag, your tender embrace, I just knew I had to have
you.
I catch myself laying here just smelling the scent of your
smell, so sexy and erotic, just your scent alone makes my
toes curl.
When I'm close to you the thought of your body that close
to mine makes me feel like a little girl.
I get butterflies just being in the same room with you every
time.
I thought only in movies, only in fairy tales do you fall in
love this fast.
My heart skips a beat whenever your name gets
mentioned.
Dangerously in love with you is what I am.
I look at you and all I can think is this man is what I want
and need.
My body lays here screaming at you, just be with me.
I daydream of cooking for you after a long day at work
rubbing your feet, giving you a massage as I transfer the
weight of the world from you to me.
Be the lucky woman to bear your last name, have your
children and give you nothing but sweet love every day.
As I lay here in your arms, I watch you so peacefully; I can't
help to wonder if you are dreaming about me.
Walks in the park on a beautiful day, us having a pretty
baby girl, she'll have your smile with my pretty face.
I just want to be the quiet for you in a world full of thunder,
just like you are for me.
I want you to see me, and just the settle smile from my
face, gives all the sunshine you need.
I can't help but lay here and watch you while you sleep so
peacefully.
Every inch of my body screaming for you, wishing I was yours and
you were mine. My king and me your queen, Adam and Eve for all
time.

Unprotected

I gave you my heart, put it in your hands to hold, and protect.
Gods plan to love and protect me until the end.
You protected me from the world, protected me from myself.
I loved you for that every day through and through.
One thing I didn't take into account was to protect myself from you.
Now I sit here broken hearted and bruised.
Can't stop crying, everything began and ended with you.
You are the one I run to for everything, my protector, provider, confidant, and my best friend
When I'm hurt, scared, or upset I run to you.
When I have exciting news, had a great day, you're the first person I run to.
You make everything better.
Make my smiles brighter, my laughter louder.
Make me smile when there is rain, make me laugh and forget my pain.
What do I do, who do I run to when my pain, my tears, my shattered world is caused by you?

Sad Love Song

I want to hate you.
To kick, punch, and scream.
Yell at you until I have no more voice.
Never speak to you again.
My flesh wants to just walk away.
My spirit, my heart gets in the way.
I understand why you are doing this trying to protect me
from long term pain.
To love someone and get hurt is a horrible thing.
When you have a love sent down from heaven for only you.
A love that was unconditional and pure, a love that was
never suppose to hurt you.
To get hurt by that kind of love is a pain, a pain that makes
you cry every day, that only your love can take away.
Take my hand, walk with me, guide me, love me and never
let go.
I don't know if you see it or not, if you know it, but we have
such an unconditional precious love.
A love that very few will ever get to know.
God made you a great man, a heavenly man; he also made
you just for me.
You are my Adam, I am your Eve.
We've lost touch over time, but always found our way back.
Never lost the love we had together, me and you is what
we've always had.
My heart, my tears are in your hands.
You give me joy, laughter, happiness, ecstasy that no other
can or ever has.
But yet you don't want to, you won't.
You will never be my man.

A Night of Intimacy

With my face in your hands you look into my eyes.
Tell me goodnight, kiss my lips so soft and sweet.
Just the simplest kiss from you seems like it only happens in the movies.
You lay me down play in my hair; run your fingertips up and down my body as I lay there.
We both watch TV, then fall asleep.
You wrap me in your arms, so close and tight.
The way a running back holds that football on a Monday night.
In your hands, your big strong arms, I'm safe, peaceful, my mind is at ease.
A perfect night of intimacy.
No sex, just you and me.

Eye Opener

She had your back, down for you no matter what.
You threw her away before you could even see her.
The loyalty you had in her is so hard to find.
She gave you unconditional love, that love is one of a kind.
Your good now because you don't know what you threw away.
In time the world, reality, life, will show you what you were missing was her.
She feels sorry for you and you don't even know it, she knows what you are throwing away.
You'll be lucky if you find loyalty, unconditional love like this again.
The whole package, you'll spend your lifetime trying to get it.
It's too bad; if you opened your eyes you could have seen you already had it.

It's Been a Long Time

Here I am running back to you again, and as always you're right there waiting, picking up exactly where we left off.
I have loved you since I was 12 years old, and there's no getting over that.
You have been loyal to me no matter what, there to listen, no matter what I had to say was good or bad.
We both know my loyalty has not exactly been the same, I have taken you for granted, and leaving you over and over just knowing you will always be there when I'm ready to come home.
You are my sanity when there is no one else to talk to.
Without you there would be no peace in my heart at all.
You put a smile on my face.
You have always been there for me, when I'm hurting you heal my heart, you listen to my pain. When I'm crying you wipe my tears away.
When I have good news you there to celebrate with me and give me all the words of excitement that I need.
Through good and bad your always there.
You're my shouting voice, when no one else can hear me.
I promise this time I will not only be true to you, but true to myself. I'm back for good and this time I promise I will never let anyone else come in between us.
I think about you every day, you're you in heart, mind, and my soul wherever I go.
This pen to this paper ignites a fire between us that no one can put out.
Just to hear your voice, to speak the words you whisper into my ears, so soft and so sweet.
Takes me to a level of ecstasy, so erotic, so sweet
You make love to me all day and night, from the inside to the outside of my body and mind.
You send chills up and down my body every time I'm around you.
Unless someone has had a taste of you, they would have no idea how you make me feel, in my body, heart, mind, and soul.
Thank you so much for being you, for taking me back.
For loving me for me, listening to everything I have to say whether it's good or bad, never asking anything in return.

This time I promise my loyalty will never leave again.
I can never give you the release you give me. My loyalty
can never compare to yours.
Please listen when I say this, I'm so sorry for not being as
good to you are you have always been to me.
I love you. I never want to live without you again.
Poetry, it's been a long time.

New Love

What did you expect?
That he would roll it off like it was cool.
Tell you he still loved you.
You broke his heart over and over, you and him are no more and you're through.
Now you have this man he wines and dines every woman he comes across.
He doesn't love you and has no plans for it.
Now all you can think of is the man with the broken heart.
Maybe this is karma getting back at you.
Maybe your new love will push through.
But all you have is time now.
Sit, wait, and hope.
Maybe one day this new love will love you the way the broken hearted man used to.

The Built of a Man

A hand is just a hand, a back is just a back, and arms are just arms.
That's what most people see.
Some women only see the muscles, the abs, and the toned body and call that sexy.
I see the true meaning of the depth of every part of your definition.
Your hand, strong enough to take mine.
Your back big and wide, strong enough to bear the weight of the world.
Your arms, to wrap me in love and keep me protected, to hold me tight.
The true meaning of every part of your definition.
The built of you, every part of you was built to protect and nurture me.
My protector, my provider.
The built of you is the definition of what you are to me.

Sista Girl

Ooo sista girl what r u going to do?
Out here all alone no one to turn to.
Scared, helpless, hopeless, no one but you.
The one you thought you loved, doesn't love you.
Sista girl what are you gonna do?
Another baby, no marriage, no man.
All alone with those kids, you just look at yourself and
shake your head.
You are smarter than this, this mess you got yourself in.
You had a plan, a good plan; you should have just stuck to
it.
Yes the world is hard but for you it just got harder.
So scared, so confused.
Sista girl what are you going to do?

No Words

A love so sweet and pure, great enough to be put on a pedestal.
Just the slightest touch felt better than anything in the world.
Being held by you literally felt like there was nothing in the world except me and you.
With a love like that, how can it hurt so bad?
How can the thought of letting go come across our minds.
No matter what, I was always yours and you were always mine.
How exactly am I suppose to say goodbye?

Dark Cloud

Just hang on she tells herself, the struggle will be over soon.
Her heart is torn, her energy is weak.
How much longer can she make it through?
She smiles to hide the pain, laugh to stop the tears that come down in the night like pouring rain.
Since she was 12 she can remember her life being a constant battle.
Fighting for that innocence of a little girl that within seconds a man can take away.
Crying out, mommy why couldn't you protect me from the pain?
She's a teenager now, she don't need mommy anymore.
She can handle herself, that's what she tells herself over and over.
Her heart is good and pour.
He came and told her everything she needed to hear, used and abused her, took her innocent trust in the most harmful way. She couldn't rid the sheets of the bloody stains.
Now all grown up, she is as beautiful as can be.
On the outside constantly smiling, on the inside crying and screaming. Dear God, please help me, give me your strength, and please don't forget me.
As a woman once again another took everything but her soul.
She just can't take this anymore.
Her life everyday walking through a dark cloud.
She sees the sun at the end of her journey.
She reaches my hand to touch it, but in between us there's too much space.
Just hang on she tells herself, the struggle will be over soon.
Right over there she can see the sun.
Please sun if you her, please shine her way.
Take away her dark rainy cloudy days.

Heartbreak Angel

How could an angel break my heart? Why didn't he catch my falling star? I wish I didn't wish so hard. Maybe I wished our love apart. How could an angel break my heart?
I believe that's how the song goes.
As it plays in my head over and over.
My ears hear what you are saying, but my heart plays the song.
I've never yelled at you before this day.
I'm screaming so loud now and you can't hear me.
I look out the window and see the pouring rain; never again will a rainy day be quite the same.
You looked me dead in my and said baby I love you, there's no reason in the world that I wouldn't be with you, except it just doesn't feel right.
The crushing blow from those words put my heart into cardiac arrest that night.
Not you, not the one sent from God, my angel can't be doing me like this.
My heart is screaming so loud for you right now, but my screams can't get passed the walls of my sound proof heart.
Even in the midst of my pain, all I want is to be in your arms.
You were sent here for me from heaven. Made just for me from God.
What's more right than that? How can that ever feel wrong?
My angel, my lover, my protector, and my friend.
How could an angel break my heart?
Someone please answer that question.

Close Your Eyes

Close your eyes, picture me standing in front of you.
You holding my face in your arms the way you do.
You kissing me so soft, slow, and gentle, and me kissing you.
Close your eyes, can you picture it?

Pillow

I went to bed wanting you last night.
Thinking about you, wanting you to hold me tight.
Tossing and turning, dream after dream.
No matter how many times I turned, fluffed, or pretended it
was you when I held that pillow of mine.
It wasn't you when I opened my eyes.

Alone

How can someone so great, beautiful, such a woman be all alone?
Lying in bed at night, no one to hold you, no one for you to hold.
The ones that want you, you do not want, just anyone won't do.
The one you truly want is nowhere around to hold you.
Does he want you, does he see you, and does he even know you are there?
So beautiful, so great, but yet laying in bed all alone, no one is there.

Good Feeling

Damn you feel so good.
Your touch, your warmth, your smile I just can't get enough
of.
I love the way you look at me as I'm laying in your arms
and you are holding me tight.
The chills and warmth I get when you kiss me on my
forehead and say goodnight.
Protector is such a strong word.
A word that I give to you.
In your arms I feel so protected, safe from the world.
Nobody to touch me, no one to hurt me, my heart is safe
and secure.
Such a great feeling, so hard to put into words.
I write poetry right I'm suppose to have a word for every
emotion I feel.
What do I do, how do I act, when the feeling is so good I
can't find the words to tell.
When you're not around my body yearns for you.
I can close my eyes breathe deep and feel the touch from
you.
Please whatever happens don't you take this feeling from
me.
I just can't lose this feeling, this good feeling from you.

Blissful Stupidity

I want to live in a bliss of stupidity.
My reality is reality.
No one else just you and me.
No one to get in the way, no one in between you and me.
You make me so happy.
In your arms I'm so safe and protected.
Blissfully happy is what you make me.
Just let me live in this blissful stupidity of no one else just you and me.

Just When

Just when I gave up on love.
You came and showed me there is still a happily ever after.
When I was falling I didn't even realize it because you were
there breaking my fall each time.
You make me smile when I cry.
Hold me tight in your arms.
Keeping me protected from the hurt of the world.
The definition of my rock, you give me strength when I am
weak.
Just when I was going to give up.
Unconditional love, happily ever after, you found me.

A Dark Night Without You

A lonely drive in the middle of the night.
This long dark road.
Imagining my world without you.
The sun is gone, you're not around.
Nothing but a never ending long dark road.
Alone and emptiness on a long dark road.
No passenger seat driver to share this journey.
The road is so dark, black, silent, and so empty.
To imagine my life without you.
It's like driving down a long dark road in the middle of the
night.

Pretty Girl

It's such a thrill, a game, a chase to get the pretty girl.
Everyone wants her, and even more, everyone wants to know who's going to get her.
Now the thrill, the chase, the game is over and gone, you won.
Now you don't want her anymore.
She's left with nothing but her mind turning with the countless conversations of hopes and dreams.
The seed you planted and watered, but didn't wait to see it grow.
She's left with nothing but a broken heart.
You're left with the championship belt from winning over the pretty girl.
You take your belt and walk away with a smile.
As she glues back the pieces of her broken heart.
The thrills of being the pretty girl.

Aphrodite

She is love, so beautiful and so sweet.
The warmth you feel from her is so tender.
When you're in the arms of the one you love you feel like a little baby.
You cry from the overwhelming feeling that she brings.
You scream to the highest mountain from the joy you are feeling.
She is beautiful, so sweet.
She can protect you from anything in the world except herself.
She can hurt like no other pain you have ever felt.
She can take you to hell and back before you even know it.
Drain you from all emotional and mental peace you have ever had.
She is love, so beautiful and sweet, but yet she can be so sad.
Her name is Aphrodite, she is the goddess of love.

Bittersweet

The slightest touch from your fingertips feels like a touch from heaven.
Your voice, makes the sound of a perfect beautiful harp.
Your intentions are so pure.
Your nature is so attentive.
Your love is sweeter than any other love before.
The joy you bring, the happiness you fill inside me.
When you hold me, your arms shelter me from the hurt of the world.
Curled up like a baby, your baby, in your arms safe and secure.
A love so beautiful.
A life that can never be.
I cherish every moment I'm with you.
I say yes, you say no.
How can something that feels so right be so wrong?

Perfect Timing

You came into my life at what could have been the worst time for you.
It was the perfect time for me.
Weak and vulnerable, you loved me past my pain.
You loved me for me and didn't even care about anything else.
At my worst time you gave me your best.
When the pain hurt to the point I thought I would break, you held my face, you whipped away my tears, and you took the load of all my pain.
Never left me standing alone in the rain.
You saw me falling, you were there to catch me, to break my fall.
You are as perfect as your perfect timing.
Now the only fall I will make is in your arms, in your heart, falling in love.

Sorry If This Might Come Off Rude

Beautiful, fine as ever, every man's dream.
Baby why are you single, he must have been stupid?
I would never let you go if you were the lady on my team.
...damn..
If I had a dollar for every time I heard those same lines,
they getting to be so tired, so for once and for all let me tell
you why.
See baby, yes you're completely right I'm a beauty indeed.
I'm a gem, a treasure, damn right you'd be stupid to leave
me.
I work, cook, and clean. I always treat my man like a king.
The fact of the matter is, men cheat.
Too often men can't appreciate a woman like me.
They can't handle my expectations, fulfill what I need.
I'm not complex, not a brat, not all caught up on myself as
you may think.
See I know I handle mine and with that being said I need
you to act like a man.
I need you to change that light bulb, you know the one I
can't reach in the hallway that's been out for two months.
If you go out, I don't mind, but why is it so hard for you to
bring your ass home and act right.
I need you to take the trash out, I cook and clean, seen
baby you can do that much.
I will treat you like a king, be loyal, the most ride or die
woman you have ever had on your team. With that I expect
to be treated like a queen.
So when you ask me why am I single. Tell me he's stupid
for letting me leave.
That's my answer in a nutshell, the expectations of me.

Sleeping Alone

Curled up like a baby on your chest.
You rub my back, your fingertips feeling like a feather up and down my body.
The most peaceful moment we can ever share.
Me curled up on you, you playing in my hair.
My body is so rested, my mind is floating in the sky.
Curled up on this perfect man, wrapped in his arms tonight.
His arms are wrapped around me to hold and protect me.
His body is my comfort, my shield to keep me safe and warm.
Wrapped up in his arms there's no thunder, there's no storms.
I can lay on top of you curled in your arms forever.
Sleeping beauty is what you turn me into.
When I lay here and think about the warmth of me laying with you.
Makes it that much harder to sleep alone.

Get it Right

I'm not your old lady, your mommy, your main chic, your baby momma, or your bitch.
These are not cute pet names to me.
I'm your lover, confidant, I'm your best friend.
Your girlfriend, your woman, your wife, your queen.
Those are all acceptable names for me.
You're not my daddy, my Papi, my old man, my baby daddy, you're not my dude.
Those names I will never call you.
You are my boyfriend, my man, my protector and provider, my husband, my king.
That is what you are to me.
Baby Don't call me out of my name, with you I will always do the same.

Perfect for Me

I may not have a video vixen body.
Not an ass as big as Nikki, not boobs as big as Dolly.
I have a big forehead to connect this beautiful thick, silky curly hair to my beautiful face.
My butt, my titties, my frame, are perfect for me.
My feet are perfect indeed, with a shoe size perfect for any.
Now don't get me wrong, I do go to the gym, but not to get skinny.
I do need to tone up, just like every woman should.
I love my size, love my curves, as my son said I'm skinny thick.
Going to the gym keeps me maintained.
I'm glad I'm not a video vixen, I'm glad I'm not barbie doll skinny.
I'm so glad I'm me.
I'm glad that from the roots that connect my hair to my scalp, down to the toes on my feet.
I'm so damn phenomenal.
Sorry if you may not like it, but I'm perfect, just for me.

Quiet Storm

The rolling thunder, a line of dark clouds in the night.
The rain pours and the clouds come in, they form a black wall over the sky.
Covering the sun, making the day turn to night.
When will my life have sun light?
In the Bible it rained for 40 days and 40 nights, but that seems to be turning into years in my life.
I ask myself time and time, will this bad storm ever end.
There's too much rain I can't go out. Trapped in this bad thunderstorm, no one can come in.
No one knows I'm home, the hallowing winds blew the light out at my front door. The dark clouds covered my bright sunny smile.
The lightning bolts pierced my heart, but the thunder is too loud no one can hear my cry for help.
I scream and I cry but there's too much rain. The rain hides the tears falling down my face.
As I lay here and hold your face as you look into my eyes. I wonder could the storm finally be over in my life.
With the touch of your finger across my face, you wiped away my tears, you stopped the rain.
You held me close you held me tight. Held me with protection, letting me know everything is going to be alright. You kept me warm from the cold in my life.
Your gentle touch, your soft voice, your attentiveness, your sweet hellos. Made it so the thunder could not be heard anymore.
You heard me through the thunder. Saw my tears through the rain.
You saw my smile through the black clouds covering me every day.
To you my smile still was bright enough to shine through the black clouds that covered me like a wall.
As we lay here I look into your eyes, your sweet smile as you look into mine.
I pray that forever with me I can take this night.
I've never felt so much calm, so much warmth, so much attentiveness, intentions so pure.
I look at you and I say to myself, finally, I found quiet in a world full of thunder. Peace within my storm.

A Girl Like Me

Did you ever know a girl so seductive and sweet?
With a heart bigger than any ocean.
Her love can't be compare to any.
Lips so soft, hair silky and smooth.
Her touch, voice, and love is as gentle as you holding your
newborn for the first time.
You've never known a girl so seductive and sweet until you
met that girl.
A phenomenal woman like me.

Happily Ever After

He's like the calm warming bright rainbow after the dark
storm.
The warm look in his eyes, you can see down to his soul.
His soft gentle touch each time his skin touches yours.
The feeling of joy he brings you is so overwhelming.
He's your king, you're his queen.
He's happily ever after.

My Prayer

Now I lay me down to sleep.
I pray the Lord my soul to keep.
If I should die before I wake.
I pray the Lord my soul to take.
As a little girl I would pray that prayer, with my heart so innocent and pure.
Now I'm all grown up, there's no more of that little girl.

Protected

Take my hand, put it in yours.
Hold me close and never let me go.
I give you my heart, protect it like you would your child.
Feel my heart beat the same rhythm as yours.
We begin to beat as one. I need your unconditional love.
Can you do that?
Can you do the one thing that no one else has ever done?
Can you protect me from the hurt in the world, protect me
from the hurt of love?
Can you take my hand, protect my heart?

PART TWO

The Inner Thoughts of the Grown & Sexy

Good Morning Kiss

In the mornings you wake before me.
As I lay here you watch me sleep.
Thinking about my beauty, my grace, how much you love me
I may not even know you are doing it, but it's the most intimate moment you have with me.
As you watch me while I sleep.
You take my hair and move it to the side.
Kiss the back of my shoulder working your way inside.
A beautiful way to wake up, such a beautiful surprise.
You get in the middle of my back and kiss me all the way down.
You've reached my arch, you kiss it while you put it in, you know that makes me wet.
A beautiful way to wake up, you kissing the arch of my back stroking me at the same time.
Now I'm wide awake, all smiles is all I can be.
You roll me over, as your deep inside, give me a kiss and say good morning, as you look me in my eyes.
I'm the luckiest girl in the world, this is how I wake up every morning from your arms at night.
The best part of waking up is you by my side.

Erotic Level of Ecstasy

Is your touch as soft as your lips?
Is your stroke as strong as your hands?
When you get inside is it hard, strong, deep, and gentle all at the same time?
I see you there, as I look into your eyes.
Can you see my body screaming from the inside?
You lay me down, I close my eyes.
You whisper in my ear, baby it's about that time.
Your tongue running across my bottom lip, now down to my breast, keep going you're not there yet.
You came across my navel, now you're almost there, I'm dripping wet.
You slowly pull my legs apart.
Kiss my ring, so gentle, so soft.
Take your mouth and suck on the lips of my pussy.
That tongue hits spots that dick just can't go.
You got me there baby, now put it in.
Go deep, take it nice and slow.
Deep in my body, until the head of your dick hits my heart.
Keep going deep and slow.
Damn you keep hitting my spot.
My attention is now definitely what you got.
Now that you have all of me, I'm so dripping wet, biting my lip, trying not to scream.
It's time to pick up the pace.
A new level of erotic ecstasy is what we got to take.
Time to switch it up, come on baby just fuck me hard.
You got me biting my lip.
I just tasted blood.
I got to let it out I got to scream, I can't hold it in anymore.
Don't stop I yell, over and over.
It's yours baby you've claimed it, you took it, now you got me screaming your name.
You got me there, I feel like I'm about to explode.
Cumming over and over on your dick.
Don't stop give it to me, more and more.
Now pull out its time for you to bust your nut.
Let me taste the combination of me and you on my tongue.
Never thought two single creams put together could make one great tasting cum.

Erotic level of ecstasy.
That's where we went, that's what we have become.

Take Me Higher

First let me say be gentle, attentive, be soft, caress me with every touch.
Lay me on my stomach, massage my back, now move my long soft sexy hair to the side
Whisper in my left ear, tell me to close my eyes.
When your eyes are closed it enhances all your other senses, leaving the slightest touch to feel so epic.
Kiss the back of my neck, take the massage candle and pour the wax down my back.
As it turns to oil massage it into my spine, on my sides, down to the arch of my back while you stroke me from behind.
You whisper in my ear, are you ok, can u handle it? As you take your time.
You put a handful of my hair in your right hand, my stomach pressed against the bed.
You take your left hand and hold mine so tight as I grip yours, with each stroke you go deeper and deeper.
Toes curling, my lip biting, sweat and oil dripping down my back, my pussy so dripping wet.
A higher level is where you have me at.
Fuck me just a little hard because I'm about to come.
You say no not yet baby and pull out.
See you never knew until now how sexual and passionate I can really become.
Until you take your fingertips barely rub them across my back, barely touching me.
Blowing on me so soft, the true definition of a gentle breeze.
You watch my body yearn, the arch in my back at its peak.
You read my body, you know I'm there.
You whisper in my ear one last time, give it to me baby.
I start to cum, the biggest orgasm, I can't even speak.
My hands grab the sheets, true ecstasy.
A higher level I've reached, one only you can take me.

Goodnight Thought

As I lay here and you are not by my side.
I replay in my head when you were here the other night.
You touch, your scent, your breath against mine.
If I replay that in my head a thousand times will it makeup
for the time you are not here by my side holding me tight?
Can I touch myself the way you touch me?
Hold my pillow the way you hold me.
Maybe I can trick myself it just might feel real.
If I close my eyes and replay it in my mind a thousand
times.

Head

Lay you down not let you move.
Not let you be in control cause tonight will be about me pleasing you.
I'd climb on top of you, kissing your chest.
While I'm doing that you can feel the heat from my pussy beating down on your body then I'd move down, grab your dick and hold It tight while I'm sucking it.
Put it in just to play with you so you can feel how wet she is by getting you off.
Id hurry and take it out, I'd move down to your sack, and suck on that.
Then suck your dick while stroking it with my hand until you cum.
I'd have you cum In-between my titties for a little bit.
I'd put your dick in my mouth so you can finish not letting you pull it out until you get ready to throw me off of you.
Me sucking you so good, no deep throat needed.
Close your eyes.
Picture me ass up face down pussy in the air wet as hell as I give you head.
Can you feel me yet?
Key ingredients of giving you head passion, sex, intimacy.

Male Bashing

Men want to tell you all kinds of shit when they dick is hard and inside your pussy.
When it's out and soft it's a whole different story.
They say women are emotional creatures yet they get emotional when you're laying up.
Pillow talk you until you fall asleep.
Telling you how much they want and need you.
That good pussy makes them men weak.
When the sun comes up and you're not face to face they got to play that game.
Trying to act like you the crazy one.
Like you made up all the late night talking, pussy beating, line feeding crap.
Little do they know, you know the game very well too.
Just like you were to him, he can mean nothing but a cut buddy to you.

Mental Stimulation

Long, short, fat, skinny.
Yea size may matter to get her off, but I need you to fuck me mentally.
I need you to get deep inside my brain like you get deep inside my pussy.
Like when your dick is so deep it hits my guts.
Don't enter my pussy with your dick, I need you to enter my ear with your words.
Stimulate my brain like you would my clit.
Your intelligent conversation that's what will make me wet.
The stimulation of your dick inside my pussy makes my legs shake.
Your stimulating conversation has my brain waves going crazy, giving me an orgasm so epic.
I don't need you to lick my pussy, stroke your dick deep inside me to get me off.
I need you to fuck me mentally, mind fucking me all day long.

April's Love

She looks so soft and innocent.
You think you'll have her before she gets to you.
Slow down my love, don't think too soon.
Like mother nature she's quiet and calm. So beautiful and strong, but then in an instance she can hit you with the power of the most deadliest storm.
Yet she's the woman of your dreams, and you don't even know it.
You see her standing there, nice long legs, nice long hair.
She turns around and her beautiful face hits you with a Mayweather blow.
Then you see that smile when she turns to you, so breath taking, the sweetest hello.
She has style and grace, cooks and cleans.
Most of all, knows how to treat you like a king.
Takes care of every single one of your needs.
Above all being selfless is her greatest beauty indeed.
You never thought you could fall in love so fast and so deep.
All you knew is this one, you can't let leave.
Acts like a real woman in public, she's the trophy you need.
Holds it down in the bedroom, she knows it's not always about her.
She knows you're the man you work hard.
Tonight she'll lay you down, trade places, relax she tells you softly in your ear.
Her tongue on every inch of your body.
She's so warm and so wet, put you inside her as she puts in all the work.
Tonight is your night, you just lay there, enjoy the motions of her hips as she calms your nerves.
She's more than just sex she's exactly what every man prays to God for.
Her love is strong her heart is as big as the entire world.
Her skin, so soft and smooth.
Her beauty and loyalty from the inside out completes you.
You fell in love with April Stone, she's a keeper.
Now not losing her is all up to you.

So Good

As I lay here thinking about you I can't help but to get wet.
Your dick is so good, you do me so good.
Your touch, your kiss, your hands so strong but yet so attentive.
I never have to tell you what to do or how to do me.
Where to touch me or how to touch me.
You know exactly when to go fast, you know when to stop and take it slow.
It's so cute how I try to do you, to make you feel the ecstasy you put in me, I climb on top and kiss your chest as my hips rotate on your dick, that's as far as you let me go.
You stop me, it's so cute you won't let yourself lose control.
The feeling I get when you grab my hair when you're about to cum.
You hold me so tight and close like you're never going to let go.
As I lay here thinking about all the parts of you, I can't help but to get wet.
You are just so damn good.

Can't Get Enough of You

Your fingertips going down my back.
Your strong hands touching me with such a gentle touch.
A feeling I can't get enough of.
You have no clue until now that you literally send chills up and down my spine.
I just shaved but yet the goose bumps you give me get me all prickly again.
The sweetest touch some may call it, but they haven't had a touch like this.
Your touch, your warmth, your soft voice, it feels like heaven.
You can make me cum without being inside me, without laying one hand on me, not touching me at all.
When you put it in my toes immediately curl, my legs start to shake, my body explodes.
What I have, it's all yours.
This feeling I can't get enough of.
When I'm with you, in your arms, near your presence, we immediately become one.
Mind, body, and spirit.
With you I'm safe, secure, I'm calm.
You are the definition of ecstasy, mentally and erotically.
You're my addiction, my drug.
The feelings you give me I can't get enough of.

Explode

I can't wait until I see you.
Until I feel your body next to mine.
You In-between my legs, holding my body tight.
Your fingertips stroking my body with a sweet touch.
You deep inside me when I get ready to cum.
You beat it up harder and harder as my body explodes.
If I saw you everyday it still wouldn't be enough.
My sweet body juices pouring as you give it to me over and over.
I can't wait to feel your kiss.
Your sweet lips, soft and gentle, pressed against my skin.
Sucking on my breast, my bottom lip.
Then you stop, I think your done, but that's only the beginning.
You won't stop until I've reached a multiple orgasm.
Only then will you be satisfied, then you go down low.
You work that tongue like no one ever has ever done on me below.
I beg for you to put it in, you start to bust.
My female organs begin to explode.
My body is pulsating, yearning until I get to see you.
Until I get to feel you throbbing inside me exploding in ecstasy.

Hello Kiss

Before you kissed me, I already kissed you.
I noticed you, before you noticed me.
Before our first hello.
You kissed my lips, caressed my breasts.
You felt my warmth down below.
Your touch was so gentle, at the same time so manly and strong.
A protector, provider when you wrapped me in your arms.
I already knew then what I know now, before you opened your mouth.
Before you ever made a sound.
I kissed you before you kissed me.
I held your face, I looked in your eyes, I gave you the passion that lives within me.
The smile you give when you look at me, your hello was so sweet.
I opened my eyes, your finally kissing me.
Please don't let this feeling, this touch, and this man ever take his arms from around me.
Just your simple kiss, your simple hello will take me to ecstasy.
Before our first hello, you were already kissing me.

Classroom Crush

When I first saw you I barely knew your name.
Saw your eyes undressing me with mine.
Your shoulders so broad, your back so strong.
All I could do was think about you putting me up against
the classroom wall.
But I barely knew your name.
Is his kiss soft?
His touch, is it gentle but like the service man he is, is it
strong?
All the girls in the classroom undress him with their eyes.
The sweetest eye candy.
I'm the lucky one, I sit by him in class every time.
Secretly crushing on him, making love to him in my mind.

No Greater Head

Ass up face down is what the song says.
Yea I love it when you're in that position, head In-between my legs.
You got my legs shaking, quivering like I'm freezing cold.
But in reality you have me so hot like a volcano ready to explode.
You eat me so good.
Pussy juices and the sound of you sucking my clit is all I can hear.
I try to tell you I can't handle it but the feeling so intense.
I open my mouth and silence just fills the air.
Then you work that tongue like nobody can or ever will.
I can't do anything but scream, this feeling is so unreal.
I start to cum, wrap my legs around your head, you take my legs, pull them back, hold me down.
I'm at the moment that climax.
I can't move, legs shaking, body quivering, biting my lip, all I can do is scream.
All that's left is for you to climb on top, come on and get In-between.

Yearning

Come hold me, rub my back like you do.
While you're doing that, rub my stomach to.
I'll hold you, kiss your face, and whisper in your ear how
much I love you.
Caress my back while your deep inside.
There's nothing more erotic than feeling your fingertips
down my spine.

Intense Love Making

Your dick the pen, my pussy the paper, my hips slow
dancing on your dick to the rhythm of the words we
create, translating the language of this love song.
Passion, intimacy, poetry.
A Combined combination that creates the most intense
moment you can ever imagine.
A moment others long for, they crave, a moment only we
were blessed to be able to make.
My body temperature rises.
Passion so intense I can't breathe.
Toes curling, my hair your pulling.
Legs shaking, body quivering.
The level of intensity is to strong.
My pussy is going into convulsions on your dick.
My body screaming as your dick strokes me with the beat
of your drum.
Your eyes staring at me, watching the motion of my hips,
your hands holding my breasts.
Your deep voice telling me this is our poem, our moment.
You take my hand, I take yours, and we begin to lose control.
My body sings the sweet love song your dick just wrote.
Your dick the pen, my pussy the paper.
Intense love making is our song, the song that you wrote.

Come Get It

As I lay here and close my eyes.
I can feel your tongue all up in my pussy.
Your dick thrusting the inside of my pussy walls.
My body is yearning, my toes are curling.
Come get it.

The Love I Don't Know

I can close my eyes and imagine the feel of you touching
me.
The sweetest, softest, most attentive and gentle feeling I'll
ever know.
When your lips touch my body, your fingertips holding my
face, I get such an overwhelming feeling, I never want to
let this feeling go.
Chills literally going up and down my spine.
My back already arched so perfectly, toes curled, just
thinking about the time.
I try to open my eyes because this feels to real.
I open my eyes and that same real feeling is still there.
The love, the touch, and the man I don't know.
Deep inside my body, he gives me mental stimulation deep
down into my soul.
I have to pack my bags.
Hop on a plane, in a car, I have to meet this man, do
anything to make this feeling real.
Until then, I'll lay here, mind and body screaming for the
love I don't know.

Sapiosexual

When you look at me what do you see?
Do you see the beauty deep inside me?
Or do you just see my long curly hair?
Big pretty eyes, or my seductive stare.
Sapiosexual is what he calls me.
My mind can take you to another world.
Total recall, virtual reality, is what your body will endure.
Can you see that when you look at me, or is your vision to blurred?

Made in United States
Troutdale, OR
11/15/2024

24820971R00046